THE BOOK OF

ROCK STARS

24 Musical Icons that Shine Through History

written by kathleen krull • art by stephen alcorn

Hyperion Books for Children
New York

With thanks to Alessandra Balzer
—K.K.

A Sabina, nobile compagna di vita,
poetica e perenne fonte d'ispirazione
—S.A.

The portraits reproduced herein are limited-edition, polychrome relief-block prints. Measuring 17 x 13 inches, they are printed by the artist on 23- x 17.5-inch acid-free paper (100-pound Mohawk Superfine).

Text copyright © 2003 by Kathleen Krull
Illustrations copyright © 2003 by Stephen Alcorn

First Edition
1 3 5 7 9 10 8 6 4 2
Designed by Gail Doobinin
Printed in Singapore
This book is set in ITC Symbol.

Library of Congress Cataloging-in-Publication Data
Krull, Kathleen.
The book of rock stars: 24 musical icons that shine through history / Kathleen Krull; illustrated by Stephen Alcorn.
    p.   cm.
Summary: An illustrated collection of twenty mini-biographies of such rock music legends as Jimi Hendrix, Janis Joplin, Bruce Springsteen, and Carlos Santana.
Includes bibliographical references.
ISBN 0-7868-1950-2
1. Rock musicians—Biography—Juvenile literature. [1. Musicians. 2. Rock music.]
 I. Alcorn, Stephen, ill. II. Title.
ML3929.K79 2003
781.66'092'2—dc21
[B]
2002191901

Visit www.hyperionchildrensbooks.com

Contents

Introduction

This book gathers famous rock stars all together on one stage.

And since few things are as personal as musical taste, every choice made for the lineup in this book might be argued over.

But everyone here has been influential in some way, and all are bright icons who changed the old ways and brought in the new. Many achieved success when they were very young. Many were restless, relentless experimenters who inspired fervent, rabid, even spiritual feelings. And all are related in interesting ways to the stars of today and tomorrow. Though many in this book are no longer alive, their music and influence go on and on and on.

These are stars who caught our attention, then got us up on the table dancing. They got us moving and even *thinking*. Some of them surpassed their own music, blooming into forces of nature, powerful in surprising ways. As icons of rebellion, many blasted away the status quo and helped to break barriers in human rights and feminism. They *glow*: stars shining in the darkness, throughout history.

In their lives, rock stars aren't always the greatest of role models, so not all parents will love this book. But many will be thrilled to share some of this music with you.

Inspired by the thought-provoking portraits created by Stephen Alcorn, I feel privileged to write for young readers about a part of music history I'm passionate about.

We offer this constellation of stars with the wish that music fills your life.

—*Kathleen Krull*

ELVIS PRESLEY

When Elvis Presley was ten, he wanted a bicycle for his birthday. His parents got him a cheap guitar instead. (The bike was too expensive.) Eight years later, he had morphed into one of the star performers of all time. He might have been a shy truck driver in private, but in the spotlight, he was a different man. His hips twitched! Pouty full lips curled into a sneer visible over the collar of his leather jacket. His hair was long and slicked back into a pompadour, and with his soulful eyes and an emotional growl, he made pulses race all over the world. At concerts, crowds went insane, breaking through police barriers to try to touch him or even rip his clothes off.

Interestingly, Elvis didn't write his own songs or even play guitar especially well. It was the way he sang. Growing up in Mississippi and Tennessee, he somehow absorbed all forms of Southern music, black and white—blues, country, bluegrass, and gospel—and blended them into his own personal style. When he was a teenager, just for fun (and as birthday presents for his mom), he began making private recordings. The owner of the recording studio was impressed and enlisted Elvis to record a few more. Radio stations were immediately swamped by requests for "That's All Right, Mama," "Blue Moon of Kentucky," and "Mystery Train." In 1956, he appeared on *The Ed Sullivan Show* (shown from the waist up, to avoid his shocking gyrating hips). One out of every three Americans watched.

He disappeared for two years, drafted into the Army, but his records kept coming. With songs like "Heartbreak Hotel," "Blue Suede Shoes," "Hound Dog," and "All Shook Up," along with 142 more *Billboard* hits, Elvis went on to become the single highest-selling performer in history.

No one had ever experienced stardom on this scale. Performing became too scary, and he retreated to the luxurious Graceland Mansion in Memphis. He emerged from his cocoon mainly to crank out two or three movies a year that were mostly forgettable, but sold huge amounts of accompanying records.

By the time he returned to live performing in 1969, playing sold-out shows in Las Vegas, he had become godlike to his fans. He wore heavy makeup, sparkly jumpsuits, and flashy capes to disguise his ever-increasing girth. It didn't matter. Adoring audiences still reached out to touch him.

It was almost as if he was too big a star for mere earth. At age forty-two, Elvis was found dead at his home, Graceland.

Yet, Elvis lives. Thousands visit Graceland every year. Hundreds make their living impersonating him. And many, many rock 'n' roll stars name Elvis as their greatest influence. **(1935–1977)**

THE BEATLES

Ringo Starr

Paul McCartney

John Lennon

George Harrison

The time was the mid-1950s and
the place was the uncool town of Liverpool, England.

Art-school rebel John Lennon mastered the guitar just enough to form a band, the Quarrymen. He met up with another guitarist, Paul McCartney, who was two years younger but who had excellent taste in music. Then Paul started bringing along his friend. George Harrison might have only been fifteen, but he knew more guitar chords than they did.

George quickly rose to lead guitarist, while Paul took over bass, and John was on rhythm guitar. For years the struggling group played nonstop in clubs, belting out songs with great flair. All of them were huge Elvis fans—"It was hero worship of a high degree," Paul once said. They also steeped themselves in Buddy Holly, Chuck Berry, Little Richard, and popular standards.

Big record companies kept turning them down—"guitar groups are on the way out." But the group never lost their confidence and even started writing their own tunes. They began dressing alike, letting their hair grow unfashionably long, and calling themselves the Beatles (Buddy Holly's group was the Crickets). In Ringo Starr, all the rage around Liverpool for his solid beat and good nature, they finally found their ideal drummer.

Some people mistook them for SAINTS or HEALERS, bringing the sick and handicapped to their concerts to be cured.

In late 1962, they were able to record their first songs, "Love Me Do" and "P.S. I Love You," by John and Paul. The melodies were catchy, the guitars energetic, and the sound had never before been heard. In a single day, they recorded all the songs for their first album, *Please Please Me*, which shot to the top of British charts and stayed there for thirty weeks.

Their first American television appearance, on *The Ed Sullivan Show* in 1964, was an earthshaking event in rock music. They were cute, and the tunes "She Loves You" and "I Want to Hold Your Hand" were exciting. Beatlemania—the insane screaming, hysteria, fainting—seized the world and didn't let go for the next six years.

Each Beatle had his own maniacally faithful fans. Some worshiped George—quiet and mysterious; John was biting and cocky, frighteningly intelligent; impish Paul could croon in the most winsome manner, and Ringo, with his oversized nose—you just wanted to take him home.

Musically, the "moptops" never took a step backward. Every recording blossomed with inventive melodies, advanced recording techniques, and complex arrangements. They became the model of a self-contained rock group that wrote and performed its own material—something of a rarity back then.

John and Paul, as a team, wrote most of the songs. Themes merged from boy–girl dramas into complex stories and deeply personal feelings. "Help!" was a genuine confession, while "Yesterday" provoked tears with a string quartet. After discovering Bob Dylan, they revealed themselves in "I'm a Loser," "In My Life," and "Nowhere Man."

Suddenly, at the height of their fame, the Beatles refused to keep performing. The public exposure was no longer fun, or even safe, and who could hear the music above the shrieking, anyway? "Being a Beatle was a nightmare," George admitted years later. Some people mistook them for saints or healers, bringing the sick and handicapped to their concerts to be cured. Others, for various crazy reasons, made death threats. Arriving in a bulletproof van in San Francisco one August night in 1966, they played their last concert and vanished into the recording studio.

What resulted was *Sgt. Pepper's Lonely Hearts Club Band*—a unified concept album that seemed to be their mightiest work. People raved that rock music had arrived as art. Again, the songs and sounds were all new—"Lucy in the Sky with Diamonds," "She's Leaving Home," "A Day in the Life."

Later, the Beatles used their fame to send positive vibes with "Hey Jude," "Let It Be," and "All You Need Is Love." "The basic Beatles message," said Ringo, "was love."

Behind the scenes, all wasn't love. Legend has it that the Beatles broke up because John was with his new wife, artist Yoko Ono, too much. But the group had begun to argue over creative direction. By *Abbey Road* (named for the street in London where their studio was), the four were seldom meeting face-to-face. They did climb the roof of their building for a spontaneous sing-along in 1969 (before the police arrived and stopped it). But this was their last group performance of any kind, and *Abbey Road* (with two songs by George as its biggest hits—"Something" and "Here Comes the Sun") was to be their final album together.

All four raced right on to interesting, sometimes astonishing, solo careers . . . but was it possible Paul was *too* sweet? John too prickly? Ringo too sentimental? George too otherworldly? More than any other rock band, the Beatles seemed a case of the sum being greater than the parts. Along their magical mystery tour, they sparked each other to reach starry heights as a group, a unit.

Hope for a Beatle reunion died forever when forty-year-old John was assassinated. In 1980, a deranged fan shot him outside his apartment building in New York City. Then George died in 2001, of throat and lung cancer.

In 2000, a collection called *The Beatles 1*, with their twenty-seven greatest hits, became the fastest- and best-selling album of all time. **Harrison (1943–2001), Lennon (1940–1980), McCartney (b. 1942), Starr (b. 1940)**

"The basic Beatles message," said Ringo, "was love."

bobDYLAN

Back in Minnesota, as an unpredictable high-school freshman in the 1950s, Bob Dylan formed a garage band called the Golden Chords. In the yearbook, he wrote that his main goal in life was "to join the band of Little Richard," a flashy black rock singer. Another favorite of his was folksinger Woody Guthrie, and at nineteen he hitchhiked to New York City to visit his idol. Within hours of arriving in Greenwich Village, he was singing in a dark, smoky coffeehouse.

Some folks didn't know what to make of him—Dylan was so moody and fierce, so frail and scruffy, curls spurting like broccoli out of his head. His voice was raw and whiny—as if he'd been up all night. People found out he wasn't a traveling hobo like Woody, but a guy from a comfortable Jewish suburban background.

But most fell under the spell of his biting political protest songs, like "Blowin' in the Wind" and "Like a Rolling Stone." His popularity with fans brought him to the attention of a record producer.

Inspired by writers he loved, Dylan looked within himself for material. He was the restless poet, journeying down the lonely highway of life toward the sunset. He would toss off brilliant observations, mysterious, with multiple meanings, gems of genius to go blowing in the wind.

Jealous of the Beatles, he got more electric, more rock 'n' roll. In one notorious incident in 1965, he played three songs at the Newport Folk Festival backed by electric guitars (instead of acoustic). Legend has it that the audience booed him off the stage, outraged at such "commercialism." Dylan kept experimenting until he was seriously injured in a motorcycle accident. He dropped out of sight for a time, raising five children with his wife, Sara, in Woodstock, New York. (One of them, Jakob Dylan, later founded and fronted the Wallflowers.)

In 1975, he set off on the Rolling Thunder Revue, a gigantic tour with his old friend, folksinger Joan Baez, plus Joni Mitchell, Arlo Guthrie (Woody's son), Roger McGuinn of the Byrds, and poet Allen Ginsberg. By then he was the most respected and influential songwriter in rock, and each night he kept fans guessing which classics he'd sing—"Mr. Tambourine Man," "Just Like a Woman," or "Positively Fourth Street."

"I'm mortified to be on the stage," he said once, "but then again, it's the only place where I'm happy." In 2002, he played again at the Newport Folk Festival, with electric guitars as well as acoustic.

This time, the multigenerational audience cheered. **(b. 1941)**

Inspired by writers he loved, Dylan looked within himself for material.

He could play equally well with the guitar behind his back, or with his teeth on the strings....

Jimi hendrix

Like a bolt of lightning, Jimi Hendrix and his red-hot guitar seemed to arrive out of nowhere. Actually, the twenty-five-year-old African American (and part Cherokee Indian) came from Seattle. And he'd been around for years, working with Little Richard and many others as a backup guitarist. He'd taught himself to play by using a broom as a guitar to imitate, among others, Elvis Presley singing "Hound Dog." Over and over, he listened to his favorites, Muddy Waters and B.B. King, and he practiced every spare minute while serving in the Army.

Hendrix seemed shy and gentle, and didn't consider himself a good singer. But one day he emerged from the purple shadows as a soloist, with his own psychedelic songs to sing. The Jimi Hendrix Experience released *Are You Experienced?* in 1967, with "Hey Joe," "Purple Haze," and "The Wind Cries Mary." It was an instant success in England—members of all the British rock bands came to hear him and worship at his feet. At Paul McCartney's urging, he went on to the Monterey Pop Festival in California. After driving the audience into a frenzy, he was an international superstar.

People who heard Hendrix play live talked about it for years afterward. Besides mastering highly accomplished finger work, he teased feedback and never-before-heard sounds from his instrument, then sculpted the results into art. He dazzled with his showmanship—he could play equally well with the guitar behind his back, or with his teeth on the strings, and, in a sizzling finale, would set his guitar on fire.

In 1969, he closed the Woodstock Music Festival with a now-classic version of "The Star-Spangled Banner." With the Vietnam War raging, people read deep meanings into his blistering interpretation. He'd been working on a new album, called *First Rays of the New Rising Sun*, when he died at age twenty-seven from drug-related complications.

Hendrix's father later was able to gain control of his son's priceless estate from record companies, with the aid of billionaire Paul Allen, cofounder of Microsoft. (Allen later started a museum devoted to Hendrix in Seattle.)

Hendrix lived on through huge amounts of material released posthumously—just about every note he'd ever played—which only added to his lustrous reputation. Fans debate which musical directions he would have pursued had he lived. But few disagree that, during his short reign as a superstar, Hendrix was the most influential rock guitarist ever. **(1942–1970)**

14

the GRATEFUL DEAD
Jerry Garcia

With his shaggy hair and kindly smile, Jerry Garcia emerged as one of the most visible figures in rock. He was the lead guitarist, vocalist, and spokesman for the Grateful Dead.

His father came to San Francisco from Spain and played clarinet in big bands and orchestras; his mother was an opera-loving nurse. Garcia flunked eighth grade (he refused to do homework) and later dropped out of high school to join the Army.

He was playing banjo in local bluegrass bands when he joined up with Bob Weir and Ron "Pigpen" McKernan. In 1965, this group evolved into the Grateful Dead—the name taken from an Egyptian prayer Garcia discovered in a book.

The always mellow Garcia seemed a symbol of how young people were going to change the world with Flower Power.

The band members moved into a communal house at 710 Ashbury Street in San Francisco. During 1967's Summer of Love, the Haight-Ashbury district became *the* destination, with the Dead providing the sound track for the "long strange trip" of the '60s. Local fans loved them for their many free concerts, pulsing with peace, love, and mind expansion. The always mellow Garcia seemed a symbol of how young people were going to change the world with Flower Power.

For many, the endless, free-form Grateful Dead concert experience was bliss. The Deadheads, some of the most faithful fans in rock history, worshiped the band, following them religiously across the country like a tie-dyed traveling circus. Bonding with the other Deadheads was as much the point as hearing "Uncle John's Band," "Casey Jones," "Sugar Magnolia," and "Truckin'."

The band flourished in an unusual universe, outside the mainstream. They encouraged fans to tape their concerts and trade them with other fans. Not until 1987 did a song of theirs—"Touch of Grey"—hit the Top Ten charts. After MTV exposure, they were playing to audiences that spanned generations. By 1994, they were earning $52 million a year from tours. They played countless benefits for environmental, health, and community causes, and donated many millions to charity.

For exactly thirty years, Garcia led the Dead through all its changes, his shaggy hair going gray gracefully. Ben & Jerry's named a scrumptious ice-cream flavor, Cherry Garcia, for him. Neckties Jerry designed were some of the best-selling in tie history. Then fifty-three-year-old Garcia was found dead in his room at a substance-abuse treatment center. Flags flew at half-mast at San Francisco City Hall.

It was the end of the Dead. **(1942–1995)**

The Rolling Stones were not cute.

The band was slightly nasty, bristly, gritty. "Rock 'n' roll is only rock 'n' roll if it's not safe," said Mick Jagger, their lead singer. He himself was a dancing, prancing, devilish figure, with amazingly large lips. Sullen Keith Richards, slithering away on lead guitar, was the hard-driving tortured artist.

The two had known each other since they were seven, discovering as teens their shared passion for the same music. Jagger was studying at the London School of Economics, while Richards was a dropout obsessed with guitars. They and Brian Jones, the third key member, spent their days haunting English record stores, searching for hard-to-find recordings by black American artists like Chuck Berry. They took the name Rolling Stones from a Muddy Waters song they loved. Along the way they acquired drummer Charlie Watts and Bill Wyman, bass player.

The Rolling Stones starved at first, but soon had audiences sweating feverishly on the dance floor at the Marquee Club in London in 1962. They started recording songs like Chuck Berry's "Come On," Lennon–McCartney's "I Wanna Be Your Man," and Buddy Holly's "Not Fade Away."

As a way of gaining publicity, they set out to be the bad-boy alternative to the Beatles, downright ugly and evil. They succeeded sensationally.

Having such luck with other people's songs, Jagger and Richards decided by 1964 to increase their share of the money and write their own lyrics and music. They soon came up with "(I Can't Get No) Satisfaction" and began calling themselves the World's Greatest Rock 'n' Roll Band.

Others tended to agree. Hit followed hit, with "Get Off My Cloud," "19th Nervous Breakdown," "As Tears Go By," "Paint It Black," "Ruby Tuesday," and "Jumpin' Jack Flash."

Jones left the band in 1969, not having contributed much lately, and a month later was found dead in his swimming pool. His death was the subject of endless rumors, but by "Honky Tonk Women" he had already been replaced by guitarist Mick Taylor. Subsequent Stones included Ron Wood and Darryl Jones.

The Rolling Stones
keith richards mick jagger

With "Sympathy For the Devil," "Gimme Shelter," and "Street Fighting Man," the group broke all box-office records during its next American tour.

The band remained megastars throughout the '70s . . . then the '80s, a bit worse for wear . . . then the '90s and beyond. Their records weren't always mega-sellers, but their concert tours always sold out. In 1999, a business magazine named them the highest-earning rock group in history. But in the process the Rolling Stones have satisfied fans with flashy rock music . . . for forty years! **Richards (b.1943), Jagger (b.1943)**

There were always a lot of snakes — he himself was the self-proclaimed LIZARD KING.

Jim Morrison hated authority. Friends guessed this was a rebellion against his strict father, a Navy admiral. After leaving Florida to study film and theater in California, Morrison told people his parents were dead (not true).

A huge reader, he was soon working more on his own poetry than on schoolwork. He formed a band with classmate Ray Manzarek, then added Robbie Krieger and John Densmore. Morrison took the band's name from *The Doors of Perception*, a book by Aldous Huxley, whose title was in turn taken from poet William Blake, one of Morrison's favorites.

Their first album, with "Light My Fire," made them stars. Manzarek's electric organ swirled madly. But the focus was always on Morrison, with his black leather pants, and his rich, deep, chilling voice. He wrote as if he were a giant eyeball, spying on places of the soul most people don't want disturbed. His lyrics, with imagery not always easy to understand, were positively sinister at times. There were always a lot of snakes—he himself was the self-proclaimed Lizard King.

In his first few performances, he avoided eye contact with the audience and sometimes even sang with his back to them. Soon he was going all out to be outrageous and would do almost anything onstage. If it was forbidden, he tried it. The fans raved, police didn't. Instead of appreciating "Waiting for the Sun," "Touch Me," "Break on Through," or "People Are Strange," they persecuted him for inciting audience riots, obscenity, and disorderly conduct.

In 1969, they accused him of revealing himself to an audience in Miami and arrested him for indecent exposure. The trial was a financial and psychological blow to the band.

Morrison, by now a figure of rich myth and legend, fled to Paris to write poetry. He published his first collection, *The Lords and the New Creatures*. Then fans mourned when he was found dead in his bathtub, only twenty-seven years old.

The number of his admirers only rose. Morrison became one of the most frequently imitated rock stars ever. To this day fans—some who had not yet been born when he died—make pilgrimages to the cemetery where he is buried, Père Lachaise in Paris, which is filled with famous poets and writers from all over Europe. **(1943–1971)**

Jim
morrison
THE DOORS

JANIS JOPLIN

When leaving the stage after a performance, Janis Joplin would flip her feet in a happy little jump. It was a direct contrast to her show, with its pain-filled howl of raw emotion, her voice honed into a shriek.

She had started out by imitating her favorite black singers, Bessie Smith and Odetta, but soon was channeling angst into her own kind of music. As soon as she could, she left her childhood home of Port Arthur, Texas, and got herself to San Francisco. A band called Big Brother and the Holding Company was happy to have her as lead singer. At the 1967 Monterey Pop Festival, she stopped the show and propelled herself into the stars with her powerful rendition of "Ball and Chain."

Then, in a move unusual for a female singer at the time, she struck out on her own. She decided to present herself as a solo rock star, with bands to back her up. Carving out a role as a gutsy woman in a very male-dominated business was often a bitter struggle. She invented Pearl, a loudmouthed, hard-boiled "red-hot mama" alter ego for the stage, the place where she was happiest. Each night she extravagantly gave herself away—"take another piece of my heart"—dripping jewelry, her wild frizzy hair festive with feathers.

Joplin lived life on the edge. She chalked up her isolation and unhappiness to growing up with few options in the 1950s in a small town. Back in Texas, people didn't know what to make of a wild girl with a wild voice. Even in big cities, she was the first female rock star anyone had seen, paving the way for many more.

Those who knew her well were not surprised when she died of drug-related causes at age twenty-seven. Soon afterward came the release of her last record, backed by the Full Tilt Boogie Band. It included "Mercedes Benz," "Get It While You Can," and "Me and Bobby McGee"—which became some of her most well-known songs. **(1943–1970)**

Carving out a role as a GUTSY WOMAN in a very male-dominated business was often a bitter struggle.

Polio struck Joni Mitchell at the age of nine.

Doctors in Saskatchewan, Canada, didn't think she would ever walk again. While recovering in a children's hospital, she found strength in serenading the other patients. Sometimes she sang at the top of her lungs. And by the time she walked out of the hospital, she was a singer.

Though her voice was like an angel's, fluid and silky, it was through her writing that people first glimpsed her. Judy Collins had a major hit with Mitchell's "Both Sides Now," while Tom Rush recorded "The Circle Game" with its "painted ponies" on the "carousel of time." Later, her "Woodstock" was a major hit for Crosby, Stills, Nash and Young.

People wanted to just label her "a hippie chick with a guitar," but Mitchell was ambitious and restless and words were her toys. In song after song, words sprouted like gorgeous flowers to create quirky landscapes.

Her first hit on her own was 1970's "Big Yellow Taxi." Then, from "You Turn Me On, I'm a Radio" to "Songs to Aging Children," she wrote songs mixing her insights with unusual chords.

She dedicated her first album to her seventh-grade English teacher, "who taught me to love words."

Something about them tickled listeners in a personal way—Bill and Hillary Clinton named their daughter after "Chelsea Morning." Many have named *Court and Spark* as their all-time favorite album, with its classic songs, "Free Man in Paris," "Help Me," and "Raised on Robbery." She described what she did as "a commentary on romantic love in the twentieth century."

Tweaking her music toward jazz, experimental, and world beat, she boldly carried on even when sales were scarce. Once she was even booed by an audience at an Amnesty International benefit concert (after they had expected the Who's Pete Townshend).

Amid rumors that complications from polio were making it difficult to perform, she reunited in 1997 with a daughter she had long ago given up for adoption. On the day she was inducted into the Rock and Roll Hall of Fame, she chose to spend it with her daughter instead.

Independent and uncompromising, Mitchell exerted a rare amount of control over her recordings. As a painter and photographer, she has even done all of her own album cover art. Respect for her keeps blooming, and today, numerous singer-songwriters, women and men, claim her as their shining star. **(b. 1943)**

**WHEN JIMMY PAGE HEARD ELVIS'S "BABY, LET'S PLAY HOUSE,"
he decided on the spot that music would be his life.** And it was. A few years later,
he was the fiery guitarist every band in England wanted. While with the Yardbirds, he looked
around for pals to start his own dream band.

He found an amazing voice in nineteen-year-old Robert Plant, who was in training to be an
accountant and singing with a band called Hobbstweedle. With John Paul Jones as its bassist
and John Bonham as drummer, the heavyweight English band Led Zeppelin came to earth in
1968.

With songs in the style of black American musicians Howlin' Wolf, Willie Dixon, and Albert
King, the band was an overnight success. Between Page's zooming, killer guitar, and Plant's
wailing vocals in the mode of Janis Joplin, they were instantly the definitive heavy-metal band,
complete with properly flowing hair.

Their monster hit, "Stairway to Heaven," shared popularity with "Dazed and Confused,"
"Black Dog," "When the Levee Breaks," and "Communication Breakdown." It wasn't that their
tunes were always crushingly loud. They also had a more gentle, mystical way with songs like
"The Battle of Evermore" and "Kashmir," in which they flirted with Celtic mythology, J.R.R.
Tolkien's *Lord of the Rings*, and musical styles from all over.

Led Zeppelin began to break the Beatles' box-office records. In concert, the band played for
up to four hours, with long, glorious solos giving Page and Plant and the others a chance to blow
away sweating fans.

They rarely gave interviews, which added to their mystique. And they only released albums,
not singles—even "Stairway to Heaven" was never released as a single, instead becoming the
most played song in the history of album-oriented radio.

In 1975, Plant suffered serious injuries in a car crash while vacationing in Greece. Two years
later, his young son died of an infection, and Plant went into seclusion. In 1980, Bonham was
found dead in his bed. Led Zeppelin vowed they could not continue without their drummer.

Page and Plant have reunited periodically for successful experiments. The three surviving
members have also played together on occasion, sometimes with John Bonham's son Jacob as
drummer. In 1990, their four-disc collection, *Led Zeppelin*, became the biggest-selling boxed set
of all time. **Page (b.1944), Plant (b.1948)**

JimmY page roBert Plant

Before Pete Townshend grew up to become rock's most athletic guitarist and leader of the Who, his parents were the ones making all the noise. During constant fights, plates and pans crashed regularly around their London kitchen.

In his early teens, Townshend found some harmony when he and his best friend, John Entwistle, started off in a Dixieland band, Entwistle on trumpet and Townshend playing banjo. Shifting into rock 'n' roll, they discovered a powerhouse singer in a factory worker named Roger Daltrey, and a fanatical drummer in Keith Moon. Partly to disguise his lack of expertise, Townshend used the guitar like a machine gun, becoming a thrashing, windmill sensation.

Townshend attended art school while the other three worked odd jobs, but soon the Who became regulars at the Marquee Club in London. That's where Townshend first snapped the neck off his guitar, possibly accidentally or out of frustration with the sound system. The crowd roared, and trashing instruments became their trademark finale.

Beside sheer loudness, the Who also had unusual songs, always innovative, and usually written by Townshend. "My Generation," "Magic Bus," and "I Can See for Miles" were early anthems, and "Baba O'Riley," "Behind Blue Eyes," and "Won't Get Fooled Again" became rock classics.

Concerts were intense. Entwistle, known as "the Ox," stood calmly, thundering on his bass, while the other three courted hospitalization. Daltrey belted out his vocals while spinning the microphone round and round like a lasso. Townshend leaped into the air with his guitar, thrusting with such a potent rhythm that the others based their playing on him, not the drums. Wildest of all was Moon, flailing away in near-total chaos. Unsurprisingly, Townshend began to lose his hearing. Still, he continually pushed the band into new territory. Many considered their crowning achievement to be *Tommy*, the rock opera about a deaf, dumb, and blind messiah who plays pinball.

When Moon died of a drug overdose in 1978, the group thought hard about disbanding, but decided to forge on. The next year, their spirits were further dashed when eleven fans at a Cincinnati concert were trampled to death in a rush for seating.

Since then, they have reunited to go on several tours, sometimes with Zak Starkey (Ringo Starr's son) as drummer. In 2002, they again went on with a tour after the death of band member John Entwistle, who was found dead in his hotel room of drug-related causes.

Before all the untimely passings, though, the Who secured its place in *The Guinness Book of Records* with the loudest performance by a rock group. **(b. 1945)**

The crowd roared, and trashing instruments became their trademark finale.

THE WHO

bob marley

Few rock stars have national holidays in their honor. On the beautiful but poor Caribbean island of Jamaica, February 6 is National Bob Marley Day.

He was born into rural poverty and left home at fourteen to pursue music in the big city of Kingston. Three years later, he recorded his first single, called "Judge Not." With a catchy Jamaican rock beat—reggae—his fierce songs gave voice to the day-to-day struggles of oppressed people.

He teamed up with childhood friends and fellow singers to form a dynamic new reggae band, the Wailers. Members included Bunny Livingstone and Peter Tosh, as well as Rita Anderson, whom he later married. Marley was the hypnotic lead singer, and audiences couldn't stop dancing. The music was infused with devout spirituality, social commentary, and encouragement to rebel. Plus it was pure fun. With tunes like "Stir It Up" and "No Woman, No Cry," Bob Marley and the Wailers could do no wrong in Jamaica.

When their song "I Shot the Sheriff" became a hit for Eric Clapton, reggae went global. As the first Third World superstar, Marley introduced Jamaican music to the world and laid the ground-work for much to follow.

Pulsing hits flowed—"Jamming," "Waiting in Vain," "One Love/People Get Ready," and "Is This Love?" They were wildly popular, not just in Jamaica, but also Africa, Great Britain, and Scandinavia. Yet the band made so little in royalties that Marley once worked in a factory for a year to support his family.

His last haircut was in 1968. After that his hair stayed in dreadlocks, as part of the Rastafari faith, the Jamaican religion that was the keystone of his life.

As famous a rock star as Marley was outside Jamaica, those at home saw him as almost godlike. On political and religious issues, ordinary Jamaicans hung on his every word. He became such a national hero that some in power even took him as a threat. In 1976 he was wounded in an assassination attempt and had to leave Jamaica for his safety.

Five years later, while jogging in New York's Central Park, he collapsed. Doctors discovered that he had advanced cancer. He released his final album, *Uprising*, and died at age thirty-six. Fans went into shock at the premature loss of the freedom-fighting entertainer. **(b.1945–d.1981)**

The music was infused with devout SPIRITUALITY, SOCIAL COMMENTARY, and encouragement to REBEL.

HIS HEROES were black American bluesmen B. B. King and Blind Lemon Jefferson.

The only triple inductee into the Rock and Roll Hall of Fame is English guitar hero Eric Clapton. He was first inducted as a member of the Yardbirds, then as part of the supergroup Cream, and lastly as a sublime solo artist.

He started out planning a life in stained-glass design. Then he was expelled from art school—for playing guitar in class—and roamed London as a street performer. His heroes were black American bluesmen B. B. King and Blind Lemon Jefferson. Clubs rushed to sponsor the talented youth, and he was on his way as the model of a serious rock guitarist. Clapton became legendary for teasing the audience with extended solos, full of anguish and virtuoso technique. He earned the nickname "Slowhand" from breaking guitar strings with his force—he'd replace them onstage while the crowd waited in awe, clapping their hands slowly.

Fans worshiped him, and the scrawled sentence "Clapton is God" was soon among the most prominent graffiti in London. He definitely wasn't writing it himself. For such a rock hero, he wasn't one to hog the stage. It took years for him to strike out on his own, and then he was promptly successful with songs like "After Midnight" and Bob Marley's "I Shot the Sheriff." A tortured lament of unrequited love, "Layla" was inspired by his obsession with George Harrison's wife, Pattie. She and Clapton eventually married in 1979—their reception was a jam with three Beatles (including the magnanimous Harrison), Mick Jagger, David Bowie, and other glittering notables. They divorced in 1988.

He seemed unsure of his solo stance, at one point lurking around as Derek and the Dominos. He also was inactive for periods, but always surfed back into view, more and more as a ballad-crooning singer. Many preferred hearing his guitar to hearing his voice, but he said: "I can't play long solos anymore without boring myself." Audiences still loved him for "Lay Down Sally," "Wonderful Tonight," and "I Can't Stand It." His biggest hit was the pain-filled "Tears in Heaven," written after his four-year-old son died in a fall in 1992.

In 1999 he auctioned off one hundred of his precious guitars. Fans pounced, and Clapton gave the money to a drug rehabilitation center he had founded.

(b. 1945)

Eric Clapton

CARLOS SANTANA

Carlos Santana came from a Mexican village so tiny it had no running water or electricity.

His father, a traditional mariachi violinist, tried to teach him violin, but Carlos preferred guitar, especially the style of American greats B. B. King, John Lee Hooker, and T-Bone Walker. By age eleven, when his family moved to the border town of Tijuana, people were paying to see him playing in nightclubs.

Later, in San Francisco, he worked full-time as a restaurant dishwasher—playing guitar as a street musician during his off time. With some help from Jerry Garcia, he formed a band. He was shy and not really the leader type, but the local musicians' union required paperwork that designated a leader. So he wrote down his name, Santana, which became the band's name.

At age twenty-two, when he played for half a million people at the Woodstock festival, the group didn't even have an album yet. They knocked the audience out with "Soul Sacrifice," written just for the event. It was a whole new, Latin-based rock sound featuring an Afro-Cuban beat, mixing congas and timbales with Carlos's spicy lead guitar. Soon after they appeared on *The Ed Sullivan Show*, and surged onto radio with "Oye Como Va," "Evil Ways," "Jingo," "Black Magic Woman," "Everybody's Everything," and "No One to Depend On."

In 1973, influenced by Hinduism, he changed his name to Devadip (meaning "the light of the lamp of God") Carlos Santana. He released several albums with specifically spiritual themes, and always his music had humanitarian messages about peace, joy, acceptance, compassion, and understanding. Later he converted to Christianity.

The group earned devotion and steady sales with its soulful, heartfelt concerts, but had no radio hits after 1982. Musicians came and went, Carlos always zooming in the lead.

Then, in 1999, Santana made what is considered the greatest comeback in rock history. The album *Supernatural* sold more than ten million—by far the group's best-selling release—and won eight Grammy Awards, including best rock album of the year.

Famous all over again, Santana continues to support a wide range of causes, including United Farm Workers, Amnesty International, Doctors without Borders, Rainforest Action Network, and the American Indian College Fund. **(b. 1947)**

DAVID BOWIE

Englishman David Bowie started out as a mime, and achieved fame as a chameleon. With eerie ease, he adapted himself to fashion and trends he could see coming, and his moves never failed to inspire the stars who came after him.

He started out as a commercial artist, spent time in a Buddhist monastery in Scotland, and formed his own mime company. To finance his art projects, he made recordings. In a fluke, one of them, called "Space Oddity," became a major hit in Britain. Bowie saw this success as a sign to concentrate on music.

"Fame" was his first number one hit in America, and dramatic rock-star fame was to follow, with "Rebel Rebel," "Golden Years," and many more. *Low* proved to be one of the most influential albums of the late '70s, as was *Heroes*, followed by *Scary Monsters*. Bowie floated on his own cloud, amid starry skies, above and ahead of everyone else.

To heighten his mystery, Bowie devised ever-more elaborate and expensive tours. He even developed new identities to mask himself in. His most famous incarnation was Ziggy Stardust, a glamorous rock star from another planet, with a backup band called the Spiders from Mars. While everyone else was dressing down in jeans, Bowie pioneered the Glitter Rock scene with fiery orange-dyed hair and flamboyant unisex clothing.

"Changes" was one of his biggest hits, and Bowie himself seldom did the same thing twice. His music was experimental, sometimes controversial, and always copied. During the rare times he was out of fashion, he was a celebrity jet-setter (marrying Somalian supermodel Iman) and a frequent actor in movies and on Broadway.

Usually on the razor-sharp cutting edge, Bowie was one of the first to take advantage of music videos. "DJ," "Fashion," and "Ashes to Ashes" were staples on early MTV, and stylish videos for "Let's Dance," "China Girl," and others came later. He also embraced the Internet early on. His multifunctional Web site provides Internet service, and he makes songs available online, sometimes exclusively.

In 1997 he shrewdly offered Bowie Bonds to investment firms on Wall Street, and backed them up with assets based on his song royalties. Another innovation, and one that brought him 55 million dollars. Meanwhile, with 2002's *Heathen*, he promises to break musical boundaries into the new millennium. **(b. 1947)**

His music was *experimental*, sometimes controversial, and always copied.

BRUCE SPRINGSTEEN

Bruce Springsteen will forever be linked to a lonely little town in New Jersey called Asbury Park. Once a thriving carnival town, it became an abandoned spot on the southern shore. He grew up near there, bought his first guitar at thirteen, formed a band at sixteen, and started playing his songs in Stone Pony and other clubs around town.

Unlike many rock stars, Springsteen was not an overnight success. For a while he was a folksinger around Greenwich Village. But it was with the E Street Band—a group of New Jersey–based musicians he'd known for years—that his songs gradually caught fire. The audiences were small cult ones before he broke through to stardom with *Born to Run*. Critics hailed him as the savior of rock 'n' roll, and his hits through the years were beloved—"Blinded by the Light," "Badlands," "Hungry Heart," "Glory Days," and "Dancing in the Dark."

His sold-out stadium shows were legendary four- to five-hour parties. He would introduce his songs with long, dramatic stories, then segue into lyrics as complicated as Bob Dylan's, with music as hard-rocking as anyone else's around. For fans, the concerts were religious experiences, or at least celebrations of all that was right about rock.

At first his songs were about girls, cars, and escaping from New Jersey. He got more thoughtful with songs like "Born in the USA," which is often mistaken as a blindly patriotic song, but is actually about a bitter Vietnam War vet. He branched out into story songs about factory workers, policemen, and migrant workers, always looking for the nobility in ordinary folks. For his simple sincerity, he was most often compared to Woody Guthrie and writer John Steinbeck.

Springsteen has said that he feels like a preacher, offering music as the ultimate comfort. On the awful night John Lennon was murdered, for example, he didn't cancel a concert, but took the stage and said, "It's hard to come out here and play tonight—but there's nothing else to do." He often sang to raise money for causes he supported, including saving local places in Asbury.

In 1993, he crafted "Streets of Philadelphia" for a film about a lawyer dying of AIDS (earning an Academy Award for Best Song).

He married Patti Scialfa, a singer in the E Street Band, and continued to live in New Jersey, but moved onto an estate. In the 2001 attack on the World Trade Center, his county in New Jersey lost more people than any other. Moved by this event, Springsteen released the album *The Rising*, in which he explored messages of loss and redemption. **(b. 1949)**

He branched out into story songs about factory workers, policemen, and migrant workers, ALWAYS LOOKING FOR THE NOBILITY IN ORDINARY FOLKS.

★

She has never been afraid to belt out a song or voice an opinion.

At age twelve, Chrissie Hynde's favorite word was "England." (She lived in Akron, Ohio.) Her favorite sentence was "I just want to play guitar in a rock 'n' roll band." She didn't know any girls who played guitar, but she was a serious fan of English rock bands: the Beatles, the Rolling Stones, the Who, and especially the Kinks and their witty lead singer, Ray Davies.

Some ten years later, she made her dreams come true. She left art school, saved up her waitress money, and bought a one-way ticket to London, England.

Achieving success took a while. She worked as a model, sold purses, and wrote about music. In 1978, a record company finally advanced her the money to audition and hire a band. It was the birth of the brilliant Pretenders, and she was its lead singer, rhythm guitarist, and songwriter. The core lineup included bassist Pete Farndon, guitarist James Honeyman-Scott, and drummer Martin Chambers. Despite various changes in the band, Hynde, the only American, has kept the Pretenders going ever since, with lasting influence on many other groups.

Her singing style is not sweet, more tough and invigorating than anything. She has never been afraid to belt out a song or an opinion. She called herself a rock 'n' roll goddess. Her series of distinctive semiautobiographical hits included "My City Was Gone"—an environmentalist protest song—"Back on the Chain Gang," "Don't Get Me Wrong," and "I'll Stand by You."

She is known for her famous boyfriends, and at one point, she had a daughter with her hero, Ray Davies. She took the baby on the road with her.

In her list of "Advice to Chick Rockers," Hynde once said, "Don't take advice from people like me. Do your own thing, always." But most women in rock couldn't help being influenced by her tough stance, the trademark scowl and heavy black eye makeup, and her versatile growling voice. She wore pants, T-shirts, and jackets buttoned up to the chin—and the minute she became an animal rights activist, the jackets were no longer leather.

A fierce voice for People for the Ethical Treatment of Animals, she once started a vegetarian alternative to McDonald's. Her will stipulates that, upon her death, PETA is to take out an ad with her photo and the caption, "Dead meat should be buried, not eaten. Take it from Chrissie Hynde." **(b. 1951)**

CHRISSIE HYNDE
THE PRETENDERS

BONO U2

FEW ROCK STARS ARE AS SERIOUS AS BONO ABOUT USING FAME AS A SWORD TO FIGHT FOR GOOD.

Born Paul Hewson in Dublin, Ireland, he was raised by a Catholic father and a Protestant mother—giving him personal understanding of the longstanding Catholic–Protestant strife.

The Irish band that would become U2 formed in 1976. Drummer Larry Mullen, Jr., posted a notice on his high school bulletin board. He wanted musicians for a group to play Beatles and Rolling Stones classics. Hewson—along with guitarist Dave "the Edge" Evans and bassist Adam Clayton—passed their audition in the drummer's kitchen. They discovered they were all Elvis worshipers. According to legend, Hewson adopted the name Bono Vox (Latin for "good voice"), even though at first his voice was pretty bad. It was his energy on stage that got U2 off to a strong start. While still in high school, they won a talent contest sponsored by Guinness Brewery.

Next, they built up a dedicated following with college students. Bono wrote the group's songs, with occasional help from the Edge. He also developed a soaring high voice, becoming perhaps one of the most recognizable in rock.

Their angry songs—"Sunday Bloody Sunday" and "New Year's Day"—tended to deal with politics and religion, not romance. Their first American hit was a tribute to civil rights leader Dr. Martin Luther King, Jr.—"(Pride) In the Name of Love." Fans heard the messages, but also vibrated to the unique sound—sweeping, atmospheric, but rigorously hard-rocking, with trademark power chords from the Edge. Fans had a wild, loose time during their increasingly elaborate tours.

Over the years, while constantly reinventing themselves musically, the band continued to preach. U2 stood for hope, faith, and love. They inspired other rock stars who wanted to make a difference, leading to the creation of benefit concerts like Band Aid and Live Aid.

Bono traveled to Ethiopia to work in an orphanage with his wife, Alison Stewart. He donated his profits from "Kiss Sarajevo," a duet with opera star Luciano Pavarotti, to war relief efforts in Bosnia. His most ambitious campaign has been to help persuade wealthy countries to cancel the debts owed to them by the poorest countries. He met with world leaders and spoke eloquently before the United Nations and the United States Congress. "I'm a pest," he has said. **(b. 1960)**

KURT COBAIN

NIRVANA

His uncle offered a choice: either a guitar or a bicycle for his fourteenth birthday. Kurt Cobain took the cheap, secondhand guitar, and was soon mastering Led Zeppelin's "Stairway to Heaven."

Growing up in trailer parks around a depressed logging town miles outside Seattle, Cobain never really got over his parents' divorce. After age eight, he lived with various relatives and was diagnosed with attention deficit disorder. He later dropped out of high school, despite excelling in art class.

He had been making up songs since age four, worshiping the Beatles and then the heavy metal of Ozzy Osbourne and Black Sabbath. While continuing to write songs and play guitar, he worked on and off as a janitor, sometimes lived in his car, and checked out library books like *All You Need to Know About the Music Business*. Then, with his friend Krist Novoselic and eventually the drummer Dave Grohl, he formed a band of his own, Nirvana.

The band started bombarding parties in Olympia with Cobain's songs, gaining a loyal following and becoming favorites on college radio stations. Screaming and thrashing, they were raw, angry, antiestablishment, and intensely unhappy with the status quo. They especially hated the stagnation represented by big music companies.

All too soon, their popularity brought them to a big music company, and *Nevermind* became a smash hit, quickly selling out. The video for its best-known song, the blistering "Smells Like Teen Spirit," went into heavy MTV rotation.

Nirvana's success took everyone by surprise, including Nirvana. They were some of the most notorious antirock stars in history. They baited their audience, spit at fans, trashed equipment right in the middle of a song like "Come As You Are" or "Heart-Shaped Box."

Although an overnight millionaire, Cobain stayed grungy. Onstage he wore thrift-store clothes, and his hair was unwashed, sometimes stained with various colors of Kool-Aid. He kept huge notebooks of his lyrics and drawings. He married Courtney Love (lead singer and guitarist for the rock group Hole) in Hawaii, and had a daughter, Frances Bean.

For his ability to create such influential music out of the shards of a sad life, people saw him as a spokesman and a symbol. His suicide at age twenty-seven shocked everyone. Two days after he died, 5,000 miserable fans gathered in Seattle for a candlelight vigil. **(b.1967–d.1994)**

He had been making up songs since age four, worshiping the Beatles and then the heavy metal of Ozzy Osbourne and Black Sabbath.

Further
■ Reading
▲ Surfing
● Listening

GENERAL READING

Christgau, Robert. *Grown Up All Wrong: 75 Great Rock and Pop Artists*. Cambridge, Mass.: Harvard University Press, 1998.

Dodd, Philip. *The Book of Rock*. New York: Thunder's Mouth Press, 2002.

Graham, Bill, and Robert Greenfield. *Bill Graham Presents: My Life Inside Rock and Out*. New York: Doubleday, 1992.

Hirshey, Gerri. *We Gotta Get Out of This Place: The True, Tough Story of Women in Rock*. New York: Atlantic Monthly, 2001.

Life magazine. *Rock & Roll at 50: A History in Pictures*. New York: Life Books, 2002.

Luerssen, John D. *Mouthing Off: A Book of Rock and Roll Quotes*. Brooklyn, N.Y.: The Telegraph Company, 2002.

Palmer, Robert. *Rock & Roll: An Unruly History*. New York: Harmony Books, 1995.

Rees, Dafydd, and Luke Crampton. *VH1 Music First Rock Stars Encyclopedia*. New York: Dorling Kindersley, 1999.

Rock: The Rough Guide. London: Rough Guides, 1999.

The Rolling Stone Encyclopedia of Rock & Roll, 3rd ed. New York: Rolling Stone Press, 2001.

White, Timothy. *Rock Stars*. New York: Stewart, Tabori & Chang, 1984.

ELVIS PRESLEY
■ Evans, Mike. *Elvis: A Celebration*. New York: Dorling Kindersley, 2002.
▲ Elvis Presley Official Web site, www.elvis.com
● *Elvis Presley*, 1956; *G.I Blues*, 1960; *Elvis* (TV-special sound track), 1968

THE BEATLES
■ The Beatles. *The Beatles Anthology*. San Francisco: Chronicle Books, 2000.
▲ Beatles Official Web site, http://hollywoodandvine.com/beatles
● *Rubber Soul*, 1965; *Revolver*, 1966; *Sgt. Pepper's Lonely Hearts Club Band*, 1967; *The Beatles* (known as *The White Album*), 1968

BOB DYLAN

- Hajdu, David. *Positively 4th Street: The Lives and Times of Joan Baez, Bob Dylan, Mimi Baez Fariña, and Richard Fariña*. New York: Farrar, Straus and Giroux, 2001.
- ▲ Official Bob Dylan Web site, www.bobdylan.com
- ● *The Freewheelin' Bob Dylan*, 1962; *Highway 61 Revisited*, 1965; *Blonde on Blonde*, 1966

JIMI HENDRIX

- Black, Johnny. *Jimi Hendrix: The Ultimate Experience*. New York: Thunder's Mouth, 1999.
- ▲ Official Jimi Hendrix Web site, www.jimihendrix.com
- ● *Are You Experienced?* 1967; *Axis: Bold as Love*, 1968; *Electric Ladyland*, 1968

JERRY GARCIA OF THE GRATEFUL DEAD

- McNally, Dennis. *Long Strange Trip: The Inside History of the Grateful Dead*. New York: Broadway Books, 2002.
- ▲ Official Home Page of the Grateful Dead, www.dead.net
- ● *Workingman's Dead*, 1970; *American Beauty*, 1970; *In the Dark*, 1987

MICK JAGGER AND KEITH RICHARDS OF THE ROLLING STONES

- Davis, Stephen. *Old Gods Almost Dead: The 40-Year Odyssey of the Rolling Stones*. New York: Broadway Books, 2001.
- ▲ Official Rolling Stones Fan Club, www.rollingstones.com
- ● *Aftermath*, 1966; *Let It Bleed*, 1969; *Sticky Fingers*, 1971; *Exile on Main St.*, 1972

JIM MORRISON OF THE DOORS

- Hopkins, Jerry, and Daniel Sugerman. *No One Here Gets Out Alive*. New York: Warner Books,1995.
- ▲ The Doors Official Web site, www.thedoors.com
- ● *The Doors*, 1967; *The Soft Parade*, 1969; *L.A. Woman*, 1971

JANIS JOPLIN

- Echols, Alice. *Scars of Sweet Paradise: The Life and Times of Janis Joplin*. New York: Owl Books, 2000.
- ▲ Joplin Official Web site, www.officialjanis.com
- ● *Cheap Thrills*, 1968; *I Got Dem Ol' Kozmic Blues Again Mama!*, 1969; *Pearl*, 1971

JONI MITCHELL

- Luftig, Stacy, ed. *The Joni Mitchell Companion: Four Decades of Commentary*. New York: Music Sales Corp., 2000.
- ▲ Joni Mitchell home page, www.jonimitchell.com
- ● *Ladies of the Canyon*, 1970; *Blue*, 1971; *Court and Spark, 1974*

JIMMY PAGE AND ROBERT PLANT OF LED ZEPPELIN

- Davis, Stephen. *Hammer of the Gods: The Led Zeppelin Saga*. New York: Berkeley Books, 2001.
- ▲ Led Zeppelin: Electric Magic, www.led-zeppelin.com
- ● *Led Zeppelin*, 1969; Untitled (known as *Led Zeppelin IV*), 1971; *Houses of the Holy*, 1973

PETE TOWNSHEND OF THE WHO
■ Guiliano, Geoffrey. *Behind Blue Eyes: The Life of Pete Townshend*. Lanham, Md.:
Cooper Square Press, 2002.
▲ Pete Townshend, www.petetownshend.com
● *The Who Sell Out*, 1967; *Tommy*, 1969; *Who's Next*, 1971; *Who Are You*, 1978

BOB MARLEY
■ White, Timothy. *Catch a Fire: The Life of Bob Marley*. New York: Owl Books, 1998.
▲ Official Bob Marley Web site, www.bobmarley.com
● *Catch a Fire*, 1973; *Rastaman Vibration*, 1976; *Exodus*, 1977

ERIC CLAPTON
■ Sandford, Christopher. *Clapton: Edge of Darkness*. New York: Da Capo Press, 1999.
▲ The Official Web site, www.claptononline.com
● *461 Ocean Boulevard*, 1974; *Slowhand*, 1977; *Unplugged*, 1992

CARLOS SANTANA
■ Shapiro, Marc. *Carlos Santana: Back on Top*. New York: St. Martin's Press, 2002.
▲ Official Web site, www.santana.com
● *Santana*, 1968; *Abraxas*, 1970; *Supernatural*, 1999

DAVID BOWIE
■ Buckley, David. *Strange Fascination: David Bowie, the Definitive Story*. London:
Virgin Publishing, 2001.
▲ DavidBowie.com: the Official Web site, www.davidbowie.com
● *The Rise and Fall of Ziggy Stardust and the Spiders from Mars*, 1972; *Young Americans*, 1975;
Let's Dance, 1983

BRUCE SPRINGSTEEN
■ Alterman, Eric. *It Ain't No Sin to Be Glad You're Alive: The Promise of Bruce Springsteen*.
Boston: Back Bay Books, 2001.
▲ Bruce Springsteen, www.brucespringsteen.net
● *Born to Run*, 1975; *Nebraska*, 1982; *Born in the USA*, 1984

CHRISSIE HYNDE OF THE PRETENDERS
■ Tharper, Ian. *The Pretenders*. New York: Ballantine Books, 1985.
▲ Pretenders Archives, www.pretendersarchives.com
● *The Pretenders*, 1980; *Learning to Crawl*, 1984; *Last of the Independents*, 1994

BONO OF U2
■ Chatterton, Mark. *U2: The Complete Encyclopedia*. London: SAF Pub Ltd., 2001.
▲ Official Web site, www.u2.com
● *The Unforgettable Fire*, 1984; *The Joshua Tree*, 1987; *Achtung Baby*, 1991

KURT COBAIN OF NIRVANA
■ Cross, Charles. *Heavier than Heaven: A Biography of Kurt Cobain*. New York: Hyperion, 2001.
▲ The Cobain Memorial, www.cobain.com
● *Nevermind*, 1991; *In Utero*, 1993; *Unplugged in New York*, 1994